Dedicated to every
Firefighting Family,
especially mine.

My Wife Nicole,
and children
Cooper, Riley, and Isabelle.

Written by Michael R. Parr
based on "A Visit from St. Nicholas" by Clement Clarke Moore
Illustrated by Jasmine Smith and Michael R. Parr
Be Fire Safe! music and lyrics by Michael R. Parr
Copyright © 2023 by Michael R. Parr

Can you find these in the story?

Halligan

Fire Alarm

Bell Cap

Axe

Chain Saw

Fire Hose

Thermal Imager

Maltese Cross

Fire Helmet

343
House Numbers

Ladder

Fire Hydrant

Mailbox

Smoke Alarm

Santa's miniature sleigh and eight tiny reindeer

'Twas the night before Christmas,

in the fire house,

not an alarm bell was ringing,

not one fire to douse;

THE HELMETS WERE HUNG BY THE ENGINE WITH CARE,
IN CASE A FIRE SHOULD OCCUR SOMEWHERE;

THE FIREFIGHTERS WERE NESTLED ALL SNUG IN THEIR BEDS,

WHILE VISIONS OF PRE-PLANS DANCED IN THEIR HEADS;

AND THE CHIEF AT HOME, AND I IN MY BELL CAP,

HAD JUST FINISHED REPORTS, BEFORE A LONG WINTER'S NAP,

WHEN OVER THE RADIO AROSE SUCH A CLATTER,

I SPRANG TO THE SPEAKER TO SEE WHAT WAS THE MATTER.

"ENGINE AND LADDER RESPOND IN A FLASH,

THERE IS A FIRE ON MAIN STREET, GET THERE BEFORE IT IS ASH."

THE HOUSE LIGHTS LIT UP LIKE NEW-FALLEN SNOW,

SO THE FIREFIGHTERS COULD SLIDE THE POLE

TO THE TRUCKS DOWN BELOW,

WHEN, AS THE APPARATUS BAY DOORS ROSE,

WHAT TO MY WONDERING EYES SHOULD APPEAR,

BUT A GLOW AND SMOKE RISING INTO THE ATMOSPHERE.

MY LITTLE OLD DRIVER CLIMBED IN,

SO LIVELY AND QUICK,

I KNEW IN A MOMENT

THAT THE SMOKE WAS GETTING THICK.

RAPIDLY THE APPARATUS ROLLED WITH FLASHING LIGHTS,

WHISTLING SIRENS, AND SHOUTING HORNS EXCLAIM,

AND I 'STRUCK THE BOX'

AS DISPATCH CALLED OUR MUTUAL AID BY NAME;

"Now, engine! Now, ladder!

Now, rescue and tower!

Sign on and respond at this late hour!"

Smoke alarms woke the family,

who knew what to do,

With two ways out,

they'd get low and go if smoke was in view;

THEY ESCAPED TO THEIR MEETING PLACE TO CONVENE,

AND CALLED 9-1-1 REQUESTING A RESPONSE TO THE SCENE.

TO THE TOP OF THE PORCH! TO THE TOP OF THE WALL!

THE FIRE WAS GROWING, AND GROWING, CONSUMING ALL!

I TOOK COMMAND AND SIZED UP THE FIRE,

360 DEGREES, FROM THE GROUND TO THE SKY,

AND ORDERED THE NEXT DUE ENGINE

TO GET A WATER SUPPLY.

FROM THE BASEMENT TO THE HOUSE-TOP

THE FIREFIGHTERS THEY FLEW,

SEARCHING WITH THE TOOLS OF THE TRADE,

A THERMAL IMAGER TOO.

A BUNDLE OF HOSE FOR ATTACK,

THEY HAD FLUNG ON THEIR BACK,

AND LADDERS WERE THROWN QUICKLY OFF THE RACK.

THE SMOKE IT ENCIRCLED THEIR HEADS LIKE A WREATH,

AND THE NOZZLE WAS HELD TIGHT,

AS THEY CRAWLED LOW UNDERNEATH.

THEY FOUND THE FIRE,

COMING WITHIN A FOOT,

AND THEIR GEAR WAS ALL TARNISHED

WITH ASHES AND SOOT;

AND THEN, ON THE ROOF, FIREFIGHTERS IN PACKS,

WITH THE SCREAM OF THE CHAIN SAW AND THE THUD OF THE AXE;

THE HEAT WAS RELEASED, AND THE FLAMES BEGAN TO RISE,

AND THE SMOKE I HAD SEEN CHANGED BEFORE MY EYES.

THE FIRE GREW QUICKLY AND TRIED TO EXTEND,

BUT THE FIREFIGHTERS KNOCKED IT DOWN,

AND WERE ABLE TO DEFEND.

Each ceiling and wall were overhauled to the stud,

And the air was ventilated to get rid of the crud.

ONE ROOM WAS FOUND,

AND IT'S DOOR HAD BEEN CLOSED,

THE SMOKE WAS BAKED ON BLACK,

BUT THE CONTENTS WERE NOT EXPOSED;

A ROOM FULL OF PRESENTS

FOR FRIENDS AND FAMILY,

A TREE FULL OF ORNAMENTS,

OF PAST CHRISTMASES HUNG MERRILY.

THE FIREFIGHTERS GOT TO ACT LIKE THE RIGHT JOLLY OLD ELF,

AS THEY SALVAGED SOME CHRISTMAS FOR THE FAMILY THEMSELF.

WITH A WINK OF AN EYE, AND A TWIST OF A HEAD,

THE FAMILY KNEW THEY HAD NOTHING TO DREAD.

THE FIRE HAD HARDLY MELTED THE SNOW

AS WE MET OUR GOAL,

AND THE JOB WAS PLACED UNDER CONTROL,

INVESTIGATORS SPOKE NOT A WORD,

BUT WENT STRAIGHT TO THEIR WORK,

AS FIREFIGHTERS PLACED THE LADDERS AND TOOLS

AWAY LIKE A CLERK.

And cleaning the dirt from aside of their noses,

The firefighters and I loaded up all the hoses;

I SPRANG TO THE TRUCK,

AS DISPATCH SOUNDED THE RECALL.

AND WE CLEARED THE SCENE,

READY FOR THE NEXT FIRE, BIG OR SMALL;

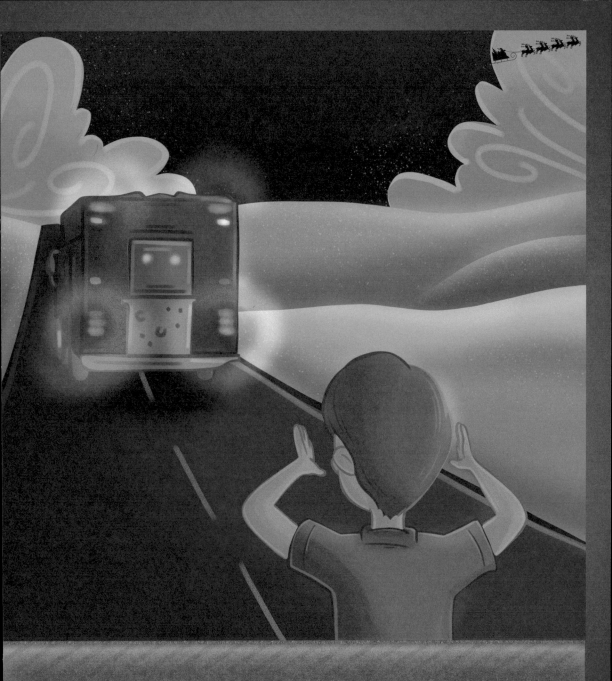

BUT I HEARD THE FAMILY EXCLAIM,

ERE WE DROVE OUT OF SIGHT,

"HAPPY CHRISTMAS TO ALL, AND TO ALL A GOOD-NIGHT!"

Even on Christmas Day,

Check your safety plan twice,

Being sure to be safe,

Is how to act nice.

Checkin' it Twice
Fire Safety

- ☐ ☐ Never Play with Fire
- ☐ ☐ Test Smoke and CO Alarms
- ☐ ☐ Make an Escape Plan
- ☐ ☐ Know Two Ways Out
- ☐ ☐ Visible House Numbers
- ☐ ☐ Close Before You Doze
- ☐ ☐ Check Doors For Heat
- ☐ ☐ Crawl Low Under Smoke
- ☐ ☐ Get Out, Stay Out
- ☐ ☐ Go to Your Meeting Place
- ☐ ☐ Learn Emergency Number
- ☐ ☐ Practice

Dear Safety Partner,

Being fire safe is the bravest thing to be. Firefighters are community helpers, just like police officers and emergency medical technicians. Firefighters assist with fire and rescue emergencies and fire prevention. You can help the community helpers by practicing fire safety. Below are fire safety messages to share with your family.

Never Play With Fire - Fire is hot, burns, and is dangerous. Don't play with fire or things that make fire like matches and lighters. Stay 3 feet away from things that are hot and can burn you. If you ever get fire on your clothes, Stop! Drop! and Roll!

Test Smoke and Carbon Monoxide Alarms - Smoke and Carbon Monoxide (CO) alarms are devices that constantly watch for hazards in your home. Ensuring they are not expired and have fresh batteries will keep your family safe. Smoke is visible, but Carbon Monoxide is invisible, tasteless and odorless. Don't disable alarms if they sound unless you are certain it is unrelated to Carbon Monoxide.

Make An Escape Plan - Talk to your family about the best ways to escape your home in an emergency, where you will meet outside, like a mailbox or the end of your driveway, and how to call for help, like 9-1-1.

Know Two Ways Out - Anywhere you go, learn two ways out. In your home it could be the bedroom door and a window. At a business it could be the front door or the emergency exit often at the back door. The best exit isn't always the way you normally go in and out. If your second exit is not on the ground floor, keep your door closed and stay at the window so firefighters can rescue you with their ladders. If you have a phone, call 9-1-1 and tell them where you are.

Visible House Numbers - After completing your escape plan, make sure firefighters can identify your home from the street with visible house numbers. Whether an apartment building or a single family home, have the building numbered and visible from the street.

Close Before You Doze - Fire needs heat, fuel, and oxygen to burn. Closing doors in your home can isolate fire and smoke as well as slow it's growth giving you more time to escape. Closing doors and placing smoke alarms in every isolated room, like a bedroom and office, will give you the greatest protection.

Check Doors For Heat - If you hear your alarms go off and have to open a door to escape, feel it with the back of your hand low to high for heat. If the door is hot, do not use that door and go to your second exit for a way out.

Crawl Low Under Smoke - If you encounter smoke as you are exiting your home, get low and go by crawling under the smoke. Smoke will rise from the heat of the fire leaving the air lowest to the floor as best for breathing.

Get Out, Stay Out - When you hear the "Beep! Beep! Beep!" Get out and stay out. Do not go back inside for pets, toys, personal belongings or other people. Firefighters have the equipment to go into a fire and you can help by telling them where someone or something may be.

Go To Your Meeting Place - Having a meeting place allows you to know if everyone got out of your home. From your meeting place you can call for help and communicate with Firefighters when they arrive.

Learn Your Emergency Number - Teach your family the best number to call for help in your community. An emergency could be a fire, a medical problem, or a crime. 9-1-1 is a nationwide program in the United States for reaching emergency services.

Practice - Train your family's response by practicing your home escape place by doing Exit Drills In The Home (EDITH). Waking up to the stress of an emergency is not the time to create or use your escape plan for the first time.

Be Fire Safe!
Sounds of Fire Safety

When you hear the Beep! Beep! Beep! You got to get out, stay out!

When you hear the Beep! Beep! Beep! You got to get out, stay out!

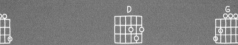

When you hear the Beep! Beep! Beep! Even when you sleep.

When you hear the Beep! Beep! Beep! You got to get out, stay out!

Chorus

I want to be fire safe! (clap clap) Be fire safe! (clap clap)

Be fire safe, (clap, clap) that's the bravest thing to be.

Verse 2

If you get fire on your clothes, you got to stop, drop, and roll!

If you get fire on your clothes, you got to stop, drop, and roll!

If you get fire on your clothes, near your shoulders or your toes.

If you get fire on your clothes, you got to stop, drop, and roll!

Verse 3

Everywhere you go, you got to know two ways out!

Everywhere you go, you got to know two ways out!

Everywhere you go, at a home, a store or a show.

Everywhere you go, you got to know two ways out!

Verse 4

If you see smoke, thick and black, you got to get low and go!

If you see smoke, thick and black, you got to get low and go!

If you see smoke, thick and black, crawl low so it's at your back,

'f you see smoke, thick and black, you got to get low and go!

A Visit from St. Nicholas by Clement Clarke Moore 1779-1863

'Twas the night before Christmas, when all through the house

Not a creature was stirring, not even a mouse;

The stockings were hung by the chimney with care,

In hopes that St. Nicholas soon would be there;

The children were nestled all snug in their beds,

While visions of sugar-plums danced in their heads;

And mamma in her 'kerchief, and I in my cap,

Had just settled our brains for a long winter's nap,

When out on the lawn there arose such a clatter,

I sprang from the bed to see what was the matter.

Away to the window I flew like a flash,

Tore open the shutters and threw up the sash.

The moon on the breast of the new-fallen snow

Gave the lustre of mid-day to objects below,

When, what to my wondering eyes should appear,

But a miniature sleigh, and eight tiny reindeer,

With a little old driver, so lively and quick,

I knew in a moment it must be St. Nick.

More rapid than eagles his coursers they came,

And he whistled, and shouted, and called them by name;

"Now, Dasher! now, Dancer! now, Prancer and Vixen!

On, Comet! on, Cupid! on, Donder and Blitzen!

To the top of the porch! to the top of the wall!

Now dash away! dash away! dash away all!"

As dry leaves that before the wild hurricane fly,

When they meet with an obstacle, mount to the sky;

So up to the house-top the coursers they flew,

With the sleigh full of Toys, and St. Nicholas too

And then, in a twinkling, I heard on the roof
The prancing and pawing of each little hoof.
As I drew in my head, and was turning around,
Down the chimney St. Nicholas came with a bound.
He was dressed all in fur, from his head to his foot,
And his clothes were all tarnished with ashes and soot;
A bundle of Toys he had flung on his back,
And he looked like a pedler just opening his pack.
His eyes—how they twinkled! his dimples how merry!
His cheeks were like roses, his nose like a cherry!
His droll little mouth was drawn up like a bow
And the beard of his chin was as white as the snow;
The stump of a pipe he held tight in his teeth,
And the smoke it encircled his head like a wreath;
He had a broad face and a little round belly,
That shook when he laughed, like a bowlful of jelly.
He was chubby and plump, a right jolly old elf,
And I laughed when I saw him, in spite of myself;
A wink of his eye and a twist of his head,
Soon gave me to know I had nothing to dread;
He spoke not a word, but went straight to his work,
And filled all the stockings; then turned with a jerk,
And laying his finger aside of his nose,
And giving a nod, up the chimney he rose;
He sprang to his sleigh, to his team gave a whistle,
And away they all flew like the down of a thistle,
But I heard him exclaim, ere he drove out of sight,
"Happy Christmas to all, and to all a good-night."

Made in United States
Troutdale, OR
12/20/2023

16250099R00024